MONSTERS

PAT HANCOCK

illustrated by
Paul McCusker

Scholastic
New York • Toronto • London • Auckland • Sydney

Scholastic-TAB Publications Ltd.
123 Newkirk Road, Richmond Hill, Ontario, Canada L4C 3G5

Scholastic Inc.
730 Broadway, New York, NY 10003, USA

Ashton Scholastic Pty Limited
PO Box 579, Gosford, NSW 2250, Australia

Ashton Scholastic Limited
165 Marua Road, Panmure, Auckland 6, New Zealand

Scholastic Publications Ltd.
Holly Walk, Leamington Spa, Warwickshire CV32 4LS England

ISBN 0-590-73169-6

6 5 4 3 2 1   Printed in Hong Kong   9/8 0 1 2/9

VAMPIRES

Vampires are neither dead nor alive. They are undead. They need fresh blood to keep them going, and usually get it by hypnotizing unfortunate people with their glowing red eyes. Vampires have to be invited in for their first snack, so their favourite victims are those who knew them when they were alive. People bitten by a vampire usually become vampires too.

Vampires only move about between sunset and sunrise. They can change shape, and often take the form of a bat, cat or rat. In human form they're tall, thin, and very pale, with blood red lips, fang-like teeth, and atrociously bad breath. They have razor-sharp finger nails curved like claws, and hair growing on the palms of their hands. Many, like Count Dracula, are elegant dressers. But because mirrors can't pick up vampires' reflections, they can't ever see how nice they look!

> *Vampires can be kept at bay with garlic cloves, crosses, thorny vines, burning torches and mustard seeds tossed on the roof. Sunlight and running water will also destroy them.*

DRAGONS

There are as many kinds of dragons as there are stories about them. Some look like long slithery serpents, others like fierce dinosaurs. A few are friendly and gentle, but most are absolutely terrifying.

These huge, scaly creatures are well suited to their role as guardians of treasure. They use their long tails and clawed feet to keep out anyone who dares approach the gold, jewels or kidnapped princesses they are hiding in their caves. Sometimes the nastiest dragons go on a roaring rampage, spewing smoke and flames from their nostrils and burning up the surrounding countryside.

Many dragons have wings, but not all of them can fly. Most of them also produce a poisonous spittle that can eat away at even the strongest armour. In the last 300 years, though, dragons seem to have lost the power to spread fear and trembling throughout the land.

---

*In Romania, people used to call dragons **draculs.** A fifteenth century Romanian prince who lived in Transylvania was nicknamed Dracula because his family's symbol was a dragon.*

MUMMIES

Mummies have been around for thousands of years, but they're newcomers to the monster scene. Until they got starring roles in Hollywood horror movies, no one but archeologists paid very much attention to them.

A mummy is not one of your better-dressed monsters. The white linen strips he was buried in come undone and stick out all over the place. With his legs all wrapped up like that, he's not very graceful either. He usually shuffles and lurches along, his arms held stiffly in front of him to help him keep his balance. If his face isn't wrapped, it looks rather dried and wrinkled — but that's to be expected of skin that's a few thousand years old! So is the strange musty smell that warns he is near.

Mummies don't eat and they don't talk. They just follow their victims until they catch them in a deadly vice-like grip. They do this because they're angry at the people who opened up their tombs. There are no recorded sightings of mummies on the loose, but some museum guards are probably a little jumpy when they have to walk through the Egyptian section late at night.

The nasty rumours about mummies seem to have started with stories of a curse on those who opened the tomb of King Tutankhamen in 1922.

KRAKEN

The kraken was the most terrifying of all the monsters lurking in the cold dark depths of the sea. It was certainly the biggest creature imaginable, and all sorts of underwater demons lived on its skin.

Some claimed it was so big that ships' crews occasionally mistook it for an island, and dropped anchor beside it. When they began to stomp about and build cooking fires on its back, the huge beast would object. Down it would dive, taking with it the men and their ship. Other stories claimed that the kraken didn't even have to dive to rid itself of pesty visitors. It simply reached up with its many arms, and brushed or pulled the sailors into the sea. Those arms were supposed to be long enough and strong enough to snatch some poor fellow perched way up in the crow's nest of a passing ship.

The kraken often surfaced just before a storm, bringing with it thousands of fish. Many people now say that it was probably a giant squid or octopus.

On November 2, 1878, a giant squid was caught off the Newfoundland coast. It had arms over 10.5 metres long, a body six metres across, and eyes that were bigger than beachballs!

ZOMBIES

Zombies are horrible creatures with glazed, unseeing eyes, who shuffle along at night in search of their victims. They can't make any decisions on their own — they must follow their master's every command. Their master is the one who makes them rise from their graves through magic spells and potions. However, these secret charms don't actually bring them back to life. They simply turn the dear departed into the "walking dead," ready to follow orders. And since only very unpleasant characters would use such spells, the orders usually aren't very nice. Often zombies are ordered to terrorize the countryside. In some cases, they're used as slave labour by a master who doesn't want to pay union wages. And since they don't eat, there's no need to give them time off for lunch either!

Some people used to believe that bakers got all their cooking done during the night with the help of zombies.

SASQUATCH

The Sasquatch is something of a puzzle. Some people say it isn't a monster at all, but simply a shy type of great ape that has learned to live in the colder climates of British Columbia, Alberta and the Yukon. Bigfoot, its American relative from the northwestern United States, could be a similar kind of ape. Native peoples and early European visitors had scary tales to tell about coming upon a Sasquatch unexpectedly.

Sasquatches are about two and one-half metres tall, and weigh anywhere from 160 to 200 kilograms. They have flat faces, long arms and huge feet and they're covered in black or brown fur. A few beige and white ones have been spotted further north. Anyone getting close enough to take a whiff says they're the stinkiest, foulest smelling critters around. They eat berries, nuts, roots or small animals, and may hibernate during the coldest months.

There have been reports of Sasquatches throwing things at people, chasing them and peeking in their windows. One man even claimed that a family of four Sasquatches held him captive for a week! Usually, though, they seem to be shy creatures that mean no harm.

In 1969, Skamania County, Oregon, passed a law that said one could go to jail for 10 years or be fined $10,000 for shooting a Sasquatch.

LOCH NESS MONSTER

Stories of water *beisties* with magical powers or nasty habits have long been a part of Scottish folklore. So it's not surprising that a mysterious monster would choose Scotland's Loch Ness as its home. Over 213 metres deep in many places, it's the perfect hideaway for a most unusual beast.

Thousands of people claim to have spotted Nessie. To some she has looked like a serpent; to others, like a type of sea otter. Most people report seeing just a bump or two moving across the lake. Their imaginations fill in the part of her that's hidden beneath the surface. Every now and then Nessie peers up out of the lake. Photos taken when she does this suggest that she has a rather small head atop a thin neck nearly two metres long. From head to tail she may reach lengths of up to nine metres.

As monsters go, Nessie is rather timid. Sudden noises frighten her off, and she manages to keep out of sight whenever big expeditions set out in search of her. Many people think Nessie is a hoax thought up in the 1930s to bring more business to the Loch Ness area. Others say she's just some logs floating on the lake. Scientists say that, if she's real, there must be others like her in Loch Ness.

There's an old prophecy which says that if Nessie is harmed the city of Inverness will be destroyed by flood and fire.

GRIFFIN

The griffin was a terrible mythical monster that was supposed to live in central Asia. It had the head and wings of a giant eagle, and the body of a huge lion. The griffin would soar through the sky like a black storm cloud, searching for people, horses, sheep and oxen to eat. When it spotted something that caught its fancy, it would swoop down from the sky and snatch up its victim in its powerful claws.

Its claws were thought to be so big that when people came across the tusks of mammoths or the horns of antelopes, they assumed these must have come from a griffin's foot. A single feather from its body was as big as a tree. People continued to believe in the existence of griffins from early Roman times right through to the Middle Ages. They were often used on shields, flags and coats of arms.

Griffin stories kept people away from gold mines and other valuable treasures they were supposed to be guarding.

COCKATRICE

All monsters don't have to be big. Some small creatures are so nasty that they belong in the monster category anyway. The evil, mythical cockatrice was one such creature. It was a small snake that hatched from an egg laid by a rooster. Anything that looked closely at a cockatrice died, even its rooster parent.

In many ways it looked just like a small yellowish snake. On its head, however, was a red rooster's comb. It also had piercing red eyes that could kill with one glance. Its breath was incredibly poisonous, and anything it touched was burned to a crisp. It left behind a trail of scorched plants and blackened animals as it slithered along the ground. Even the bravest of knights could not destroy the cockatrice. The instant he tried to run it through with a spear, his arm would turn into a useless piece of charred flesh, and within seconds, he would be dead. Only someone armed with a mirror could destroy this horror: made to see its own reflection, it too would drop dead!

Tales about the basilisk, another mythical monster, are almost identical to those about the cockatrice.

YETI

For hundreds of years people living in Nepal and Tibet have told tales about a mysterious creature lurking in the mountains. Recorded sightings in Nepal go back over 200 years. The monster had many names, but the most common one was yeti. A reporter writing about it in 1930 gave it the name Abominable Snowman.

Huge footprints in the snow are often the only evidence that the yeti might exist, but even Sir Edmund Hillary reported seeing such footprints as he scaled the Himalayas. Those who have actually seen the yeti claim it reaches heights of nearly three metres and has such long arms that its wrists reach its knees. Its head is slightly cone-shaped and its body is covered with reddish-brown hair everywhere but its face. One person claims to have seen a pale yellow yeti.

The yeti is a smelly creature and its breath is especially foul. Home is supposed to be a gorilla-like nest or a den in the rocks. Some local people believe seeing a yeti brings bad luck. There are also stories about these creatures snatching children from neighbouring villages. However, some scientists think that yetis aren't abominable at all, but simply relatives of great apes they haven't yet identified.

> *Scientists who study animals that may or may not exist are called cryptozoologists.*

CYCLOPS

The Cyclopses were huge mythical monsters who worked as servants for the Greek god Zeus. They made thunderbolts for him, and fought his enemies.

They were hideous creatures, with only one eye peering out from the middle of their foreheads. They were also very strong. They could carry trees on their shoulders, and often walked about swinging clubs as big as a ship's main mast. Breaking off a mountain top and hurling it at an enemy was all in a day's work. When they weren't busy serving Zeus, they lived in huge caves, where they kept sheep and cows. To keep their animals in at night, they simply rolled huge boulders in front of the openings to their caves. Whenever they were hungry, they picked up a victim — animal or human — and crunched it whole, bones and all.

The Greek hero, Odysseus, escaped from the clutches of a Cyclops by blinding it and sneaking past it when it couldn't see.

WILD MEN

During the Middle Ages, people told lots of stories about strange, hairy men who looked and acted more like animals than humans. Their bodies were covered with dark fur everywhere but on their faces, hands and feet. Some of them had tails and horns too.

These wild men were taller than the average person. Some had legs as big as trees. They were also very strong and quick. They usually roamed around without any clothes on, but a few of them preferred to wear short skirts made of leaves. Some wore animal skins in the winter.

Wild men lived deep in the forests, where they survived on fruit, nuts and the raw flesh of animals. Paintings often show them carrying huge clubs or spears. At first, they were seen as the meanest of creatures, with very nasty tempers. People thought they would carry off humans and have them for dinner. In later years people were a bit more sympathetic towards them — but still made sure to stay far away from the woods they were supposed to haunt!

Wild men and wild women were supposed to be the only ones who could capture unicorns and ride them like horses.

OGOPOGO

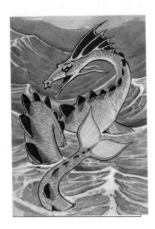

For centuries, west coast Indians have told stories about seeing a dreadful monster in British Columbia's Lake Okanagan. Some even used to throw chickens or pigs into the lake to keep the monster from attacking them.

There are many descriptions of Ogopogo. Some say he's a large whale-like creature about 30 metres long. Others say he looks like a huge log that seems to come alive and swim away faster than a person can row. Still others say he resembles a serpent with a head like a horse or sheep wearing a beard. However, most people who claim to have seen him say he is a thin, curvy animal about half a metre wide and between 10 to 20 metres long. Hardly anyone claims to have seen his head. When Ogopogo sinks below the surface, big waves move toward the shore as if a huge stone has been dropped into the lake. Many people say Ogopogo doesn't exist, but the people of Kelowna would probably disagree with that idea. They have a sign in their city warning monster hunters that Ogopogo is protected by law.

One way to tell if Ogopogo is near is to watch the birds and fish. They're supposed to panic and behave strangely when the lake demon approaches.

WEREWOLVES

Werewolf stories are nearly 2000 years old. They were most popular during the Middle Ages when starving wolves were driven to attack people at the end of a hard winter.

A person could turn into a werewolf if a spell had been cast upon him. He could also change into this monstrous beast if he wore a belt made of wolf fur, ate roasted wolf flesh, smelled or wore the plant called wolfbane, drank rain water that collected in a wolf's footprints, or was bitten by another werewolf.

The change from human to werewolf was impressive. Hair began to grow all over the person's body, and his head took on the shape of a wolf's. His teeth grew longer and pointier, and his fingernails and toenails turned into claws. Within minutes he was loping about on all fours and howling like the leader of the pack. This transformation was supposed to take place when the moon was full. By morning, the werewolf changed back to his human form — but he kept any injuries he got during his night as a wolfman. Only a silver bullet would destroy him.

There are also tales of werebears, weretigers, and even werehippopotamuses!

GORGONS

The Gorgons were three hideous sisters with clawed hands made of brass and huge golden wings. Two of the sisters — Euryale and Stheno — were as large as elephants, and had long white tusks sticking out from their faces. But Medusa, the third sister, was the most terrifying. Although she had a pretty face, her hair was a hissing, slithery mass of snakes.

There were hundreds of stone statues all around the Gorgons' cave. These were the work of Medusa. Her eyes had incredible power — just one look from them turned a person into stone. Perseus, a hero of Greek myth, managed to sneak up on Medusa and kill her by looking at her reflection in his shield instead of directly at her.

Perseus cut off Medusa's head and took it away with him in a bag. When he pulled it out later, his enemies turned to stone even though the Gorgon was dead.

GIANTS

Stories about giants are popular all around the world. Most giants are at least two and one-half metres tall, but there seems to be no limit to how tall some of them can be. They're so strong that they can pull up trees with their bare hands, toss boulders up in the air as if they were baseballs and squeeze water out of stones.

Very few giants are friendly. Most of them are only too happy to beat up or devour people whenever they get the chance. They even get into fights with each other, and the earth shakes when they do.

Giants usually live in caves or camp out in the forest. A few of them manage to renovate castles stolen from kings, to suit their huge size. Even when they live indoors, they aren't very tidy. They toss bones on the floor and rarely do their dishes. Perhaps that's because most giants aren't very clever. They can often be tricked into letting their prisoners escape or into giving up their treasures.

*Greek myths tell of huge men called **Gigantes**, with feet in the shape of serpents. They caused volcanoes and earthquakes.*

MANIPOGO

Manipogo is another one of those monsters that pop up occasionally in large lakes. His home is Canada's Lake Manitoba. First recorded reports of his presence in the lake began around 1910, but native peoples were talking about him long before that.

Manipogo looks like a big black snake to many observers, but at least one person described him as being yellowish-brown and slimy in appearance. He moves through the water like a giant caterpillar, hunching his back up and down as he goes. Manipogo is estimated to be over 12 metres long and about 30 centimetres thick. Like other lake monsters, he can move very quickly, outswimming a small boat driven by a 10 horsepower motor. He must also be very shy because he always keeps out of sight when monster hunters go looking for him.

Another "pogo" monster is Igopogo. It's supposed to live in Ontario's Lake Simcoe.

PHANTOM KANGAROOS

It's hard to imagine a huge kangaroo hopping across the midwestern United States, but that's exactly what people say has been happening ever since the early 1930's. Eyewitnesses usually report seeing a large, bouncy critter zipping across the road in front of them or causing a disturbance outside their homes. However, follow-up searches for the unusual visitor from down under reveal no evidence that a kangaroo has been in the neighbourhood, and no local zoos report any missing marsupials.

In October, 1974, police in Chicago answered a call from a man saying a kangaroo was hopping all over his front porch. That's exactly what they found when they arrived at his home. They chased the creature into an alley, but it fought them off with its hind legs and hopped away to safety. Other Chicago residents reported seeing the kangaroo over the next few days, but no kangaroo was ever caught. Through the years, people in Indiana, Ohio, Wisconsin and Colorado have also spotted the ghostly jumper. On some occasions it's been blamed for the killing of sheep, dogs and chickens.

A phantom puma has been reported many times in the area of Surrey, England, but no evidence of its presence has ever been found.

ROC

The monstrous roc seems to have been the biggest bird imaginable. Its eggs were so large that they were mistaken for the domed tops of far-off buildings. Even newborn rocs were huge, and so were their appetites. Legend has it that mother rocs brought elephants back to their nests to feed to their babies.

In one of the tales in *A Thousand and One Arabian Nights*, Sinbad the Sailor disturbs a pair of rocs. Squawking with fury, the monsters fly out over the sea carrying huge stones in their gigantic claws. One after the other, they drop them on his ships. After several bombing missions, the rocs succeed in sinking one of the boats.

Travellers returning to Europe from the Far East brought back many stories of this mighty creature. Some also brought back huge feathers that had supposedly come from a roc.

In many parts of the world people believed that huge Thunderbirds made thunder and lightning by flapping their wings.

TALOS

Talos was a mythical giant who guarded the island of Crete from invaders. Because he was made of brass, he was much stronger than any flesh and blood giant could ever be. He was kept alive by a liquid called ichor, which flowed through the single vein in his body running from his neck to his heel.

Three times a day, Talos would run around the entire island. If he spotted an invading ship approaching, he would drive it away or sink it by hurling huge rocks at it. He could also make himself red hot whenever he wanted to by lying down in a fire. Then he could burn up anything simply by touching it.

Talos eventually went berserk. Every day he raced around Crete, sinking any and every ship he saw until Crete was cut off from the rest of the world. Talos was finally tricked into drinking a magic potion that made him drowsy. A great archer got close enough to shoot an arrow at him that loosened the nail in his heel. Out it fell, and out poured the life-giving ichor. In a few minutes, Talos was nothing more than a huge brass statue lying lifeless on the ground.

> *Movie-makers still like to imagine metal men who go berserk. Often these take the shape of awkward robots who begin to think for themselves.*

BUNYIP

The Australian aborigines used the word *bunyip* to refer to several different animals they couldn't identify, but the word was also used to name a mysterious creature that was occasionally blamed for drownings. This animal was supposed to live in the lakes, rivers and water holes of Australia. In some cases, it was nothing more than a terrifying roar coming from a nearby lake. In others, it was a large furry thing rising up unexpectedly from a misty marsh. However, there have been enough similar descriptions reported to get some idea of what a bunyip might look like. It seems to have been no bigger than a young colt, with a head and face that looked like a dog. It was covered with dark fur, and had fins well-suited to swimming. Such a description makes one think of a seal. That's what many people think this strange creature must have been — a type of seal that had adapted to living in fresh water.

"Searching for the bunyip" is an expression used in Australia to mean trying to do the impossible.

FRANKENSTEIN'S MONSTER

This monster was the creation of author Mary Shelley. In her 1818 novel, *Frankenstein*, Shelley writes of a mad scientist called Doctor Frankenstein piecing together a man-like creature from various parts of stolen bodies. The monster he creates is unusually tall, with pale skin and dull yellow eyes. He can talk, and is really quite smart, but isn't anywhere close to the superman Dr. Frankenstein hoped to create. He's an evil thing, a killer driven mad by the fact that everyone he meets finds him repulsive.

The movie versions of this monster look very different from the original book version. His head is square, almost box-like, and is covered by ugly scars. His hands and feet seem huge, and he moves about in a very clumsy way. He has lost the intelligence he had in Shelley's book, and his ability to speak clearly. Not knowing his own strength, he often kills those he wants to love.

Frankenstein is the doctor's name, not the monster's. The first Frankenstein movie was made in 1910.

TERRIBLE WILD MONSTER

This monster without a name was supposed to have lived near Jerusalem in the 1720's. It wasn't very big — only about the size of a horse — but was one of the most terrifying beasts ever described. It had a lion's head and teeth, a pair of bull's horns on its forehead and an eagle's beak growing from the end of its nose.

Its body was covered with hard, pearly scales. On its back were two serpent-like wings and on its feet were huge, curved talons. It had short pointy spikes growing from the tip of its shoulders down to the ends of its hind legs.

This disgusting creature was supposed to have killed hundreds of people, cows and horses near a forest about 25 kilometres from Jerusalem. It was finally destroyed by a brave soldier who ran his lance down its throat.

At one time people were eager to buy "genuine" monster claws — which were really just rhinoceros or antelope horns collected by travellers to faraway lands.

KING KONG

Creatures such as the yeti and the Sasquatch may very well be some kind of giant ape that no one has properly identified yet. But the biggest ape of all is strictly a movie monster that exists only on film or video tape. He is Kong, the king of the jungles of Skull Island. Normally a mean, angry monster, Kong's heart melts when he meets Ann, a beautiful young actress he can hold in the palm of his hand.

Kong is captured and brought to New York to be put on display as the eighth wonder of the world. But he doesn't take kindly to being locked up in a cage, especially when he misses his new friend, Ann. He finally breaks out, stomps about the city until he finds Ann, and climbs with her to the top of the highest building in New York. It takes all the power of the air force to finally shoot him down.

> *Godzilla is another movie monster who crushes people and buildings under his huge lizard-like feet. In one horror movie King Kong and Godzilla battle it out.*

MERMEN AND MERMAIDS

Today, sea or "mer" people are usually thought to be friendly, rather romantic creatures, but this wasn't always the case. For over 6000 years, people have told stories about strange beings that have the heads and bodies of humans, but are fish-like from the waist down.

Some of these creatures helped sailors find their way to safety; others lured them to their deaths on rocks battered by huge waves. Many of them didn't do much more than show up every now and then, but their unusual appearance usually caused quite a commotion and made some sailors think twice about going back out to sea.

One of the strangest of these marine monsters — the Monk Fish — was supposedly captured off the coast of Norway in the 16th century. Its body was covered with scales, and it had fin-like arms and a fish's tail. Its head, however, looked just like a monk with his face partially covered by his hood.

Mermaids liked to sit on rocks combing their hair. A person could gain power over a mermaid by stealing her cap or her belt.

MOTHMAN

Mothman is a modern monster, sighted in West Virginia in 1966 and 1967. He was just over two metres tall, and had red eyes that seemed to glow in the dark. He also had huge grey wings which he used for flying when he wanted to move about faster than his legs could carry him.

Many people claimed to have seen this creature, who was so named because of his wings. Some of them saw him lying on the ground, others saw him shuffling along a deserted road, and still others watched in horror as he flapped his wings and took off straight into the air like a human helicopter. One teenager described how he swooped down towards the windshield of her car. Four others told how he flew above their car, keeping up with them even when the car reached speeds of 160 kilometres per hour.

Some scientists suggest that Mothman may really have been a large rare bird called a sandhill crane. It's grey with a red forehead, and has been known to fly after people.

MOKELE MBEMBE

For nearly two centuries, people have claimed that a dinosaur-like creature still lives in Central Africa. People who tell of seeing Mokele Mbembe describe a monster that sounds very much like a miniature version of Brontosaurus.

It's usually sighted near marshes or swamps, or along the banks of rivers. It has a long tail and a very long neck, with a head that looks a bit like the head of a snake. Its smooth, shiny skin ranges from greyish-brown to dark brown. Its length has been estimated at about 10 metres, and its front legs are shorter than its hind ones.

There's one report of hunters killing one of these beasts in 1959 because it was scaring the fish and the fishermen of Lake Tele in the Congo.

Some people believe it's dangerous even to speak of Mokele Mbembe. Villagers who ate meat from the one killed in 1959 were all said to have died.

MINOTAUR

The legendary Minotaur was horrible to behold. It had the body of an incredibly strong man and the head of a raging bull. Its dull yellowish hide was tougher than shoe leather. It gored its victims with its mighty horns before devouring them.

The Minotaur lived in the centre of a maze in the palace of Crete's legendary King Minos. The maze was called the Labyrinth. No one was supposed to be able to escape from it alive.

Each year seven maidens and seven young men were brought from Athens to Crete to be offered as sacrifices to the Minotaur. One year Theseus, the son of the King of Athens, volunteered to be one of the seven young men. With the help of Princess Ariadne, King Minos's daughter, Theseus reached the middle of the maze, where he fought the Minotaur for a long time. When the monster tired, Theseus grabbed it by the horns and broke its neck, silencing forever its bloodcurdling roars.

On the Isle of Crete archeologists uncovered the ruins of a palace with maze-like chambers, thought to be the original Labyrinth.

WORM MEN

Worm Men live beneath the earth in a kingdom that is also home to dragons and basilisks. They look like humans from the waist up, and like huge worms from the waist down. Their skin is scaly, like a snake's. They have long, pointy noses and tiny beady eyes. Males' faces are red; females' faces are yellow.

These creatures usually slink along the ground, but they can also use their hands to push themselves up into the air and leap forward. After a tiring day spent digging tunnels, they like to return home to a meal of roasted slugs. They are often attacked by their deadly enemies — giant toads who ride fast-moving worms.

Human visitors are destroyed unless they agree to become worm creatures. However, no one seems to want to agree to this change!

SPHINX

The ancient Greeks told stories of a vicious monster called the Sphinx. From the waist up, the Sphinx looked like a woman. The rest of its body was that of a huge lion. Two large wings rose stiffly from its back.

The Sphinx had a rather nasty habit. Whenever travellers passed its cave, it would leap out in front of them and ask them a riddle. If they gave the wrong answer, it pounced on them and gobbled them up or heaved them over a cliff. The riddle was very difficult. Since no one got it right, the Sphinx always had plenty to eat.

Finally a Greek hero named Oedipus managed to destroy the Sphinx by solving the riddle. The minute the monster heard the right answer, it roared fiercely, then turned and threw itself over a cliff.

The Sphinx's riddle: What creature has four legs in the morning, two at noon and three in the evening, and is weakest when it has most?

(Answer: Humans — when infants, they crawl on all fours; when adults, they walk; when old, they use a cane.)